THE SESAME STREET GAMES

Pictures by Peter Panas

This educational book was created in cooperation with Children's Television Workshop, producers of Sesame Street. Children do not have to watch the television show to benefit from this book. Workshop revenues from this product will be used to help support CTW educational projects.

STREET GAMES

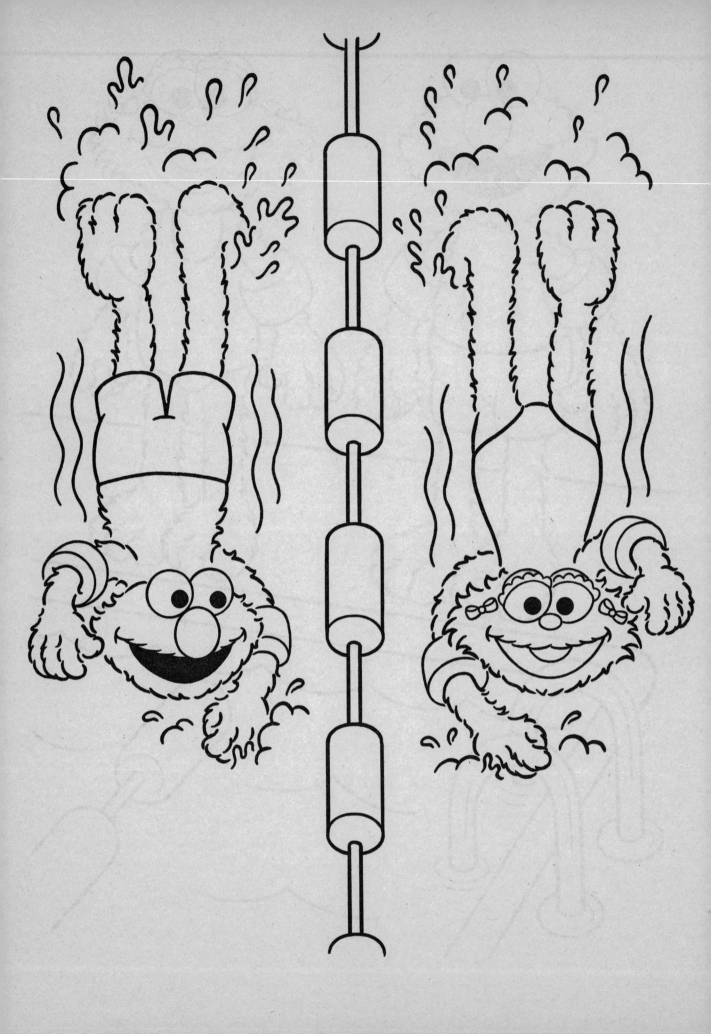

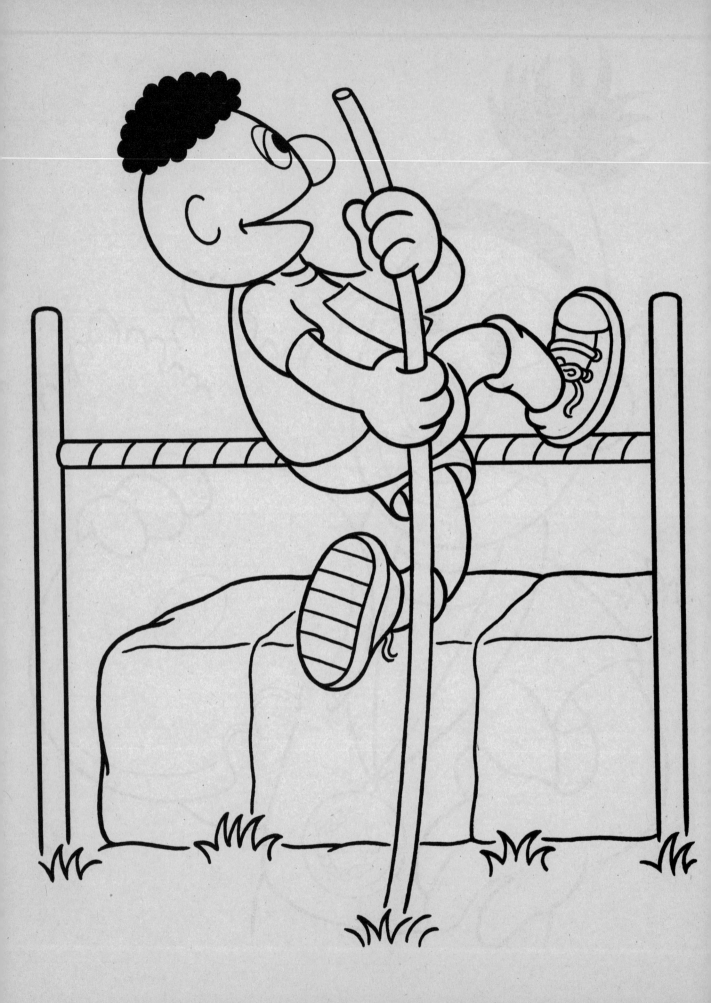

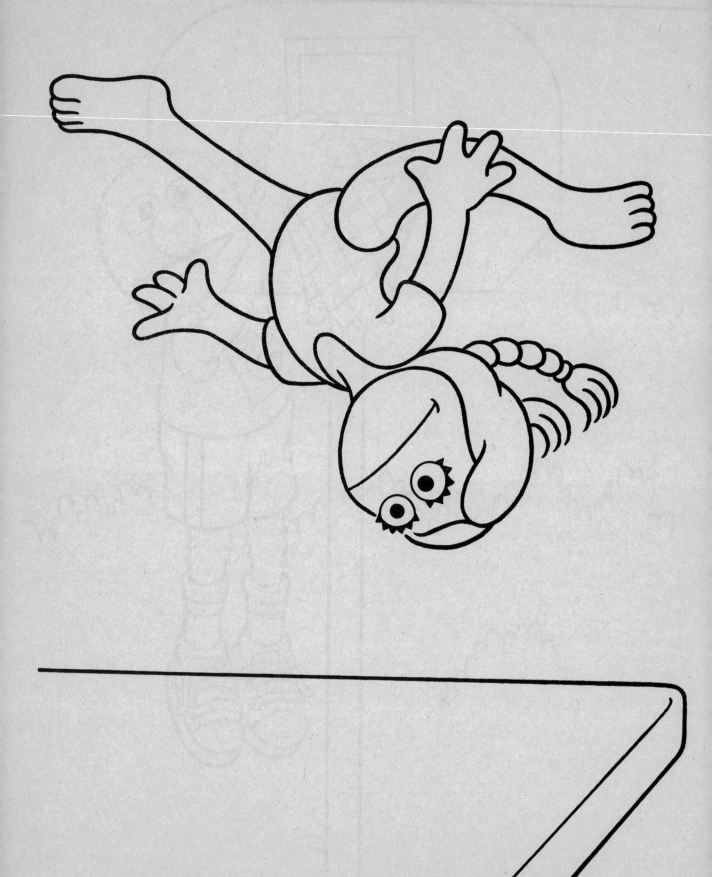

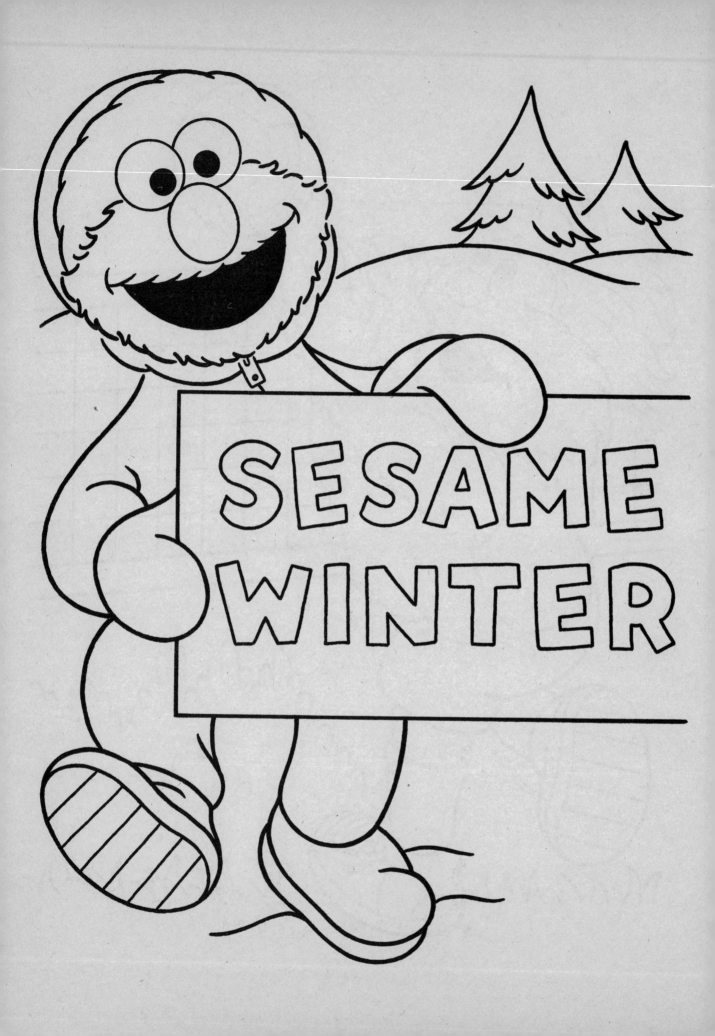

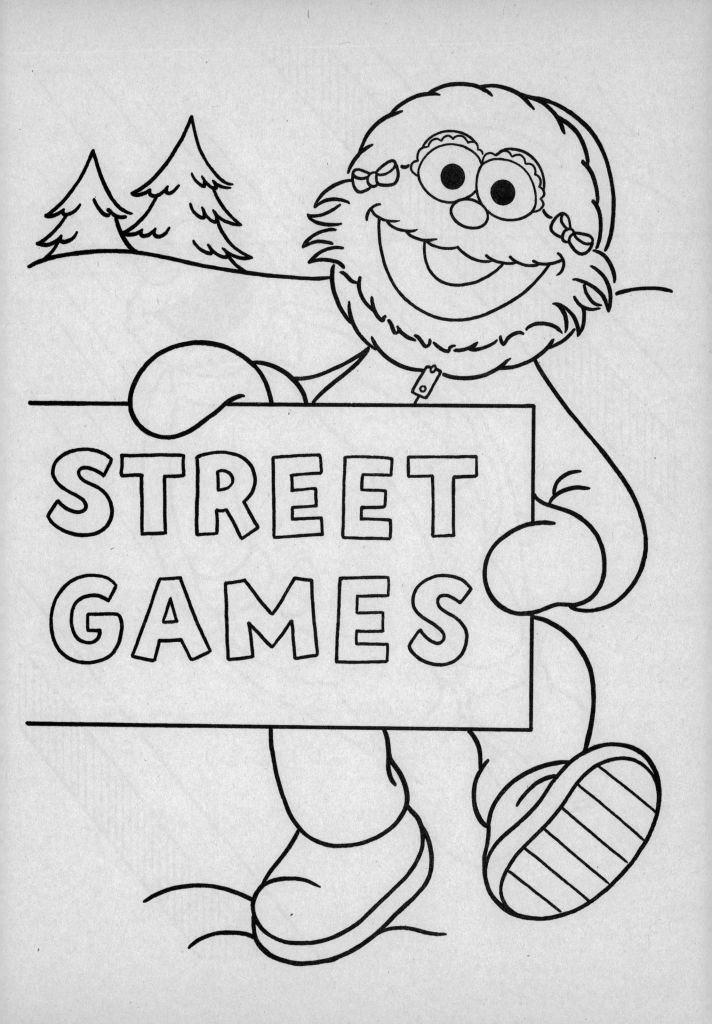

STREET
GAMES